DJ
x

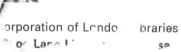

For Jamie and his "sweet teeth" – *M. P.*

For Keek and Lucy – *J. D.*

SIMON AND SCHUSTER

First published in Great Britain in 2004 by Simon & Schuster UK Ltd,
Africa House, 64-78 Kingsway, London WC2B 6AH.

Originally published in 2004 by Simon & Schuster Books for Young Readers,
an imprint of Simon & Schuster Children's Publishing Division, New York.

A CIP catalogue record for this book is available from the British Library upon request.

Book design by Mark Siegel.
The text for this book is set in Utopia.
The illustrations for this book are rendered in coloured pencil, acrylic, dye and ink.

ISBN 0689872933

Printed in China

10 9 8 7 6 5 4 3 2 1

Sweet Tooth

By Margie Palatini

Illustrated by Jack E. Davis

SIMON AND SCHUSTER
London   New York   Sydney

his is Stewart.

Your typical, average, everyday kid.

Except – for one thing.

"Iii oo-er ere."

Ahh, yes. There it is all right.

The molar at the back.

You're probably saying, "A tooth? What's so special about a tooth?"

And ordinarily you would be correct. . . . But this is no ordinary tooth.

Oh no.

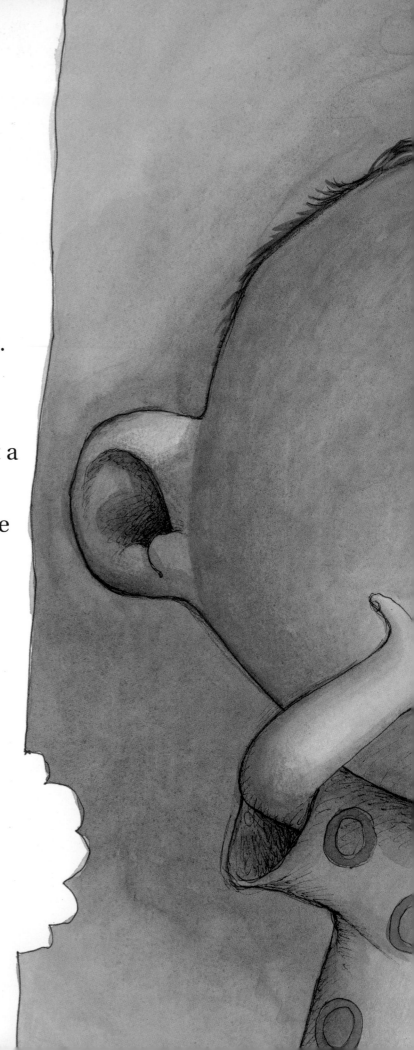

This is Stewart's sweet tooth. One nagging, annoying, demanding –

"BLAH. BLAH. BLAH. STOP YOUR WAFFLING. I NEED A CHOCOLATE BAR. NOW!"

– very loud, sweet tooth.

"DOES IT HAVE THAT GOOEY STUFF IN THE MIDDLE? BECAUSE IT'S GOT TO HAVE THAT GOOEY STUFF IN THE MID-DLE!"

"There," said Stewart through a chomp and a gulp. "Satisfied?"

"AHHHHH . . . S-WEET!"

Yes, a tooth that wants what it wants, when it wants it. And . . . lets everybody know about it.

Take, for example, two years ago at cousin Charlotte's wedding . . . .
Stewart was on his best behaviour. His shoes were shined. Bowtie
straight. Hands were spotless. Grandfather had just lifted his glass
to toast the bride and groom when . . .

**"I'm falling asleep here! Come on. Hurry up, Grandpa. Cut the cake.
Time to cut the cake. I want the end chunk with all that iiiiii-icing."**

"I don't know him," uttered Mum through a gritted smile.

"He doesn't belong to me," said Dad under his breath.

"Who is that boy?" muttered Grandmother.

Stewart wiped the pink rose from his lips. "It's The Sweet Tooth."

It was not a pretty picture.

The Tooth was no better behaved in school. Stewart had enough detention slips to wallpaper his room. Why, just two weeks ago . . .

"Who can tell me the capital of Latvia?" asked Mrs Finnegan in geography class.

"Jelly beans," said a muffled voice from the back of the room.

"Did you say something, Stewart?" asked Mrs Finnegan.

"Licorice."

"Stewart, I'm afraid I can't hear your answer," said Mrs Finnegan.

"Lollipops."

"You're going to have to speak up, Stewart."

"Hey! I'm dying here for a couple of CHOCOLATE POPCORN BITES, OK!"

Detention slip number 432.

"But, I'm telling you, it's not me," said Stewart as he was led away to the headmaster's office. "It's The Tooth!"

The cinema?

You don't really want to go there, do you? . . . Not with Stewart, anyway.

"Would somebody pass the jelly babies before I go crazy!"

"SHHHHHHHHHHHHHH!"

"Don't look at me," chewed Stewart. "It's The Tooth."

And of course, there was the unforgettable Easter basket fiasco.

Now that was really ugly.

That Sunday morning the family awoke to find jelly beans littering the living room. Marshmallow chicks were missing.

The trail of crumpled yellow wrappers led to one person, and one person only.

"Ooooh, Stewart," cried Mum and Dad in dismay.

"I can't look," whimpered his sister, Alison, closing her eyes.

"Those chocolate bunnies never had a chance," moaned Stewart, rubbing his churning stomach. "It was The Tooth."

"HEY! CAN WE STOP GOING DOWN MEMORY LANE HERE AND OPEN UP THAT BAG OF COOKIES?"

"That's it. I've had enough!" cried Stewart.

"ENOUGH? I HAVEN'T EVEN HAD ONE."

"No more cookies!" shouted Stewart. "No more chocolate. No more cake. No more nothing!"

"That's no more anything," said The Tooth. **"And . . . WHO DO YOU THINK YOU'RE KIDDING, KID? Bring on those chocolate chips!"**

Stewart sighed.

What choice did he have? He was a boy with one big, demanding sweet tooth. He tore open the bag. He grabbed one, then two – three – four cookies. He opened his mouth.

"COME TO DADDY!" shouted The Tooth.

Stewart stopped.

"What are you waiting for, kid? Come on. Cookie. Cookie. Cookie. COOKIE."

Stewart dropped the cookies. But . . . not in his mouth.

"It's over, Tooth," said a suddenly determined Stewart. "I'm cutting you off. Starting right now. It's cold turkey."

"Cold Turkey? Yuck! I hate cold turkey . . . unless you add a little cranberry sauce."

"Didn't you hear me, Tooth?" cried Stewart. "I said it's over. From now on there's nothing for you but a . . . a . . . a . . ." Stewart gulped, "healthy diet."

"Healthy? Kid, say you don't mean it," wailed The Tooth.

But Stewart meant it, all right. He meant every word. Yes, it was trying. Yes, it was difficult. OK, it was practically impossible. But Stewart stayed strong.

For The Tooth it was a different story.

"PEAS? YOU'RE GIVING ME PEAS? LITTLE GREEN VEGGIE MARBLES? Broccoli? You're feeding me a shrub? THAT'S NOT GOING TO DO IT. DESSERT! WHERE'S DESSERT? I'm begging you. WHEN DO WE GET TO THE GOOD STUFF?"

"I can't hear you," said Stewart, putting down his fork and placing his hands over his ears. Strong. He stayed strong.

"Just one teeny-weeny CHOCOLATE-COVERED PEANUT before hitting the sack. How about it? . . . A nosh. A nibble. A mint. Something!"

"Forget it," said Stewart, turning off the light. Strong. Strong.

"COME ON. WHADDAYA SAY? ONE SPOONFUL OF SUGAR," urged The Tooth. Stewart shook his head.

The Tooth was losing its grip and it knew it. **"A DROP OF CHOCOLATE MILK. One measly little cake crumb."**

"No way," said Stewart. Very strong.

"HEY, WATCH THAT TOOTHBRUSH," shouted The Tooth. **"AND KEEP THAT TONGUE OF YOURS ON THE OTHER SIDE OF YOUR MOUTH. TRYING TO WIGGLE ME OUT OF HERE, ARE YOU? Well, I'm not going, kid. I'm not going anywhere! Are you listening to me?"**

Stewart brushed. Flossed. Gargled.

"U-u-ugh," moaned The Tooth, weakly. **"He's not listening to me . . . I'll get you for this, kid."**

Stewart smiled. He was winning. Oh yes, he was winning.

Three days passed. The Tooth was quiet. Very quiet. Almost too quiet.

But Stewart wasn't thinking "tooth". He was thinking baseball.

It was the biggest game of the season. Bottom of the ninth. Stewart was at the home plate. Runners were on second and third base. Two outs. Two strikes.

The crowd was on their feet. The game was on the line. Stewart's team was down by one run. The pitcher went into his wind-up. There was a hush from the stands. A big fat fastball was heading for the plate. It was all up to Stewart. And then . . .

"BOY, COULD I GO FOR A HUNK OF BUBBLE GUM RIGHT NOW!"

Swing! Swish!

"Heh-heh-heh."

"Strike three!" yelled the umpire. "Y'er out!"

"Gotcha!" said The Tooth. **"Now, go and get me some goodies!"**

"I'll get you goodies," mumbled Stewart, dropping the bat.

Home he marched. Into the kitchen. Straight for the fridge. He yanked open the door. Rustled through the vegetable drawer. He flung lettuce. He tossed tomatoes. He hurled a head of cauliflower. And then he pulled out – a carrot. That's right. A carrot.

"It's over for you, Tooth," announced Stewart defiantly, lifting the carrot above his head.

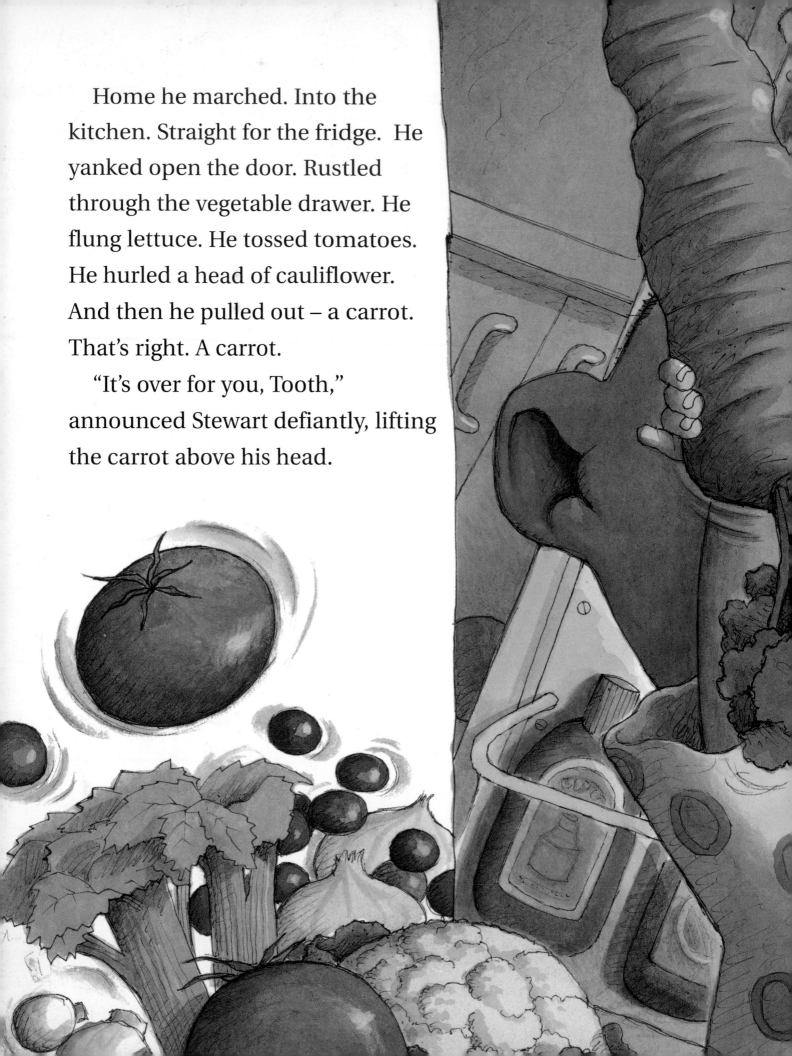

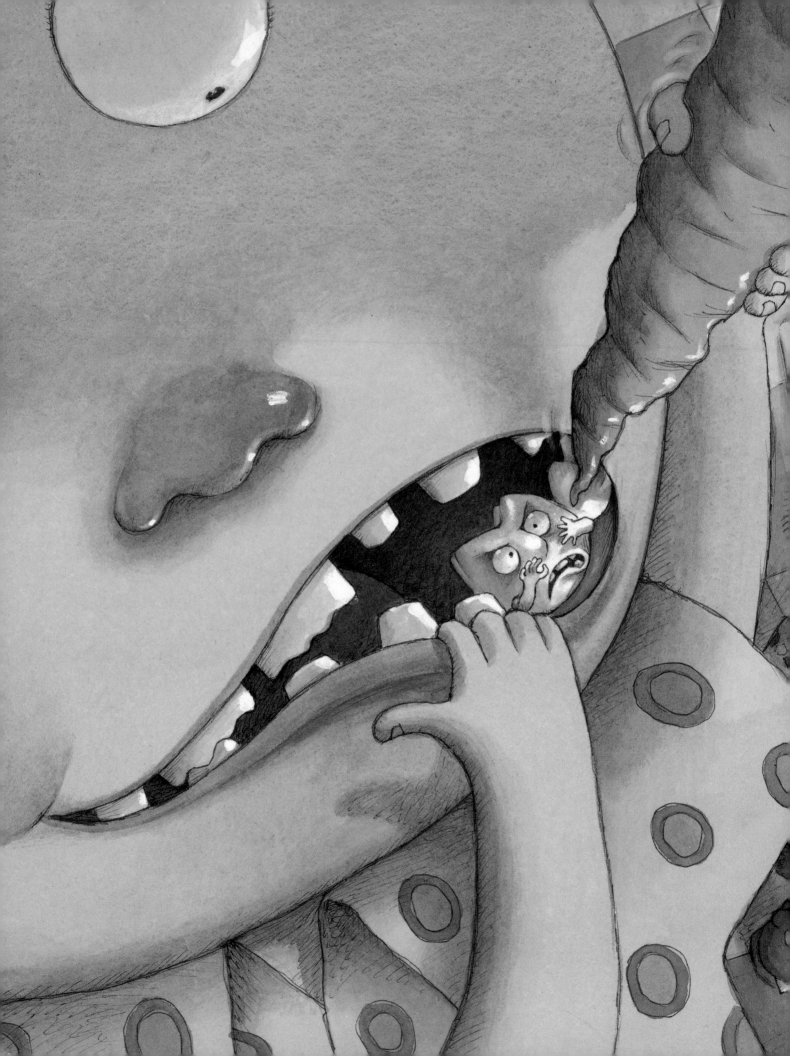

"What are you going to do with that?" asked his wide-eyed sister.

Stewart grinned. He opened his mouth wide. Very wide.

"KID! NO! NOT THE CARROT! NOT THE CARROT!"

"Yes. The carrot!" shouted Stewart.

"No, kid, no!"

Alison covered her eyes. "Am I too young to be watching this?" she asked.

Closer. Closer. Closer. And then – *CR-CR-CRUNCH*.

"Ahhh-ahh-ahhhhh. . . . So long, sweet world! . . . What a way to go. . . . Done in by a root vegetable."

Stewart rubbed his jaw. He stared at the carrot . . . and The Tooth.

It was over.

"What's going to happen to it?" asked Alison as she followed her brother upstairs to his bedroom.

Stewart placed the molar under his pillow then looked at his sister.

"Who knows?" he said with a big smile. "That's the tooth fairy's problem now."

"WAH! WAH! WAH!" cried the baby teeth.

"WOOF!" yapped the canine.

"Please be quiet," said the wisdom tooth, *"I'm trying to read."*

"PIPE DOWN, WISE GUY! WHAT DOES A SWEET TOOTH HAVE TO DO TO GET AN ICE-CREAM SUNDAE AROUND HERE? WITH HOT FUDGE! And throw some sprinkles on it while you're at it."

The tooth fairy just shrugged her shoulders. "ROTTEN TEETH!" she smiled.